LOOK AND FIND®
Santa

Illustrated by Jerry Tiritilli
Cover illustration by Alyssa Mooney

Louis Weber, C.E.O.
Publications International, Ltd.
7373 North Cicero Avenue
Lincolnwood, Illinois 60712

Ground Floor, 59 Gloucester Place
London W1U 8JJ

Customer Service: 1-800-595-8484
or customer_service@pilbooks.com

www.pilbooks.com

ISBN-13: 978-1-4127-6922-8
ISBN-10: 1-4127-6922-1

Everyone loves to decorate for Christmas! And of course, "yours truly" appears in many wonderful decorations. Check out this craft show — I'm a hot item this year! See if you can find me in all these crafts. Don't forget to find the real me, too!

2 Santa cookies

A Santa stocking

A Santa lamp

A Santa pillow

A wooden Santa doll

A Santa wreath

A Santa quilt

Santa in a centerpiece

How do I know not to bring you the same toys your parents are giving you? I visit toy stores and watch what people buy! Toy stores are almost as busy as my workshop at the North Pole — kids are always getting lost there. First, try to find me. Then see if you can find these lost children.

Bobby the Kid

Mini-Muscles, the Wonder Baby

Drummond Bugle III

I. Wright Ticketts

Lil' Topknot

Mona Lisa Murphy

Chuckles and Giggles, the twin clowns

Presto Change-o

Hi Long Leggs Jr.

One of my favorite things about Christmas is that I get to visit with girls and boys who come to see me at shopping malls. Shopping malls can be pretty crazy at Christmas, though! I'm taking a break right now. Can you find me? Can you find these crazy Christmas shoppers, too?

Curly Wiggs

Kringles the Klown

Tarzan

M.T. Pocketts

Mother Goose

Moe Hawk

Candi Cotton

Leif Eric's son

Christmas is only a few days away. And if you think it's busy at your house, you should see my workshop! Do you think I'll be ready for my Christmas Eve ride? After you find me, help me find these toys to fill my sack. We'd better check the list twice!

A ball

A red wagon

A train

A skateboard

A doll

A tricycle

A teddy bear

A truck

ORNAMENT MACHINE

OFF

ON

DART BOARDS

'Twas the night before Christmas,
and all through these houses,
People were still up,
including some mouses!

Well, this isn't *exactly* the way my
favorite poem goes, but my way is
more realistic! See if you can find
me, and then see if you can spot
these Christmas Eve classics.

A mouse
not stirring

4 children
nestled all snug
in their beds

This stocking
hung by the
chimney with care

Sugarplums
dancing

2 fathers in
sleeping caps

Cookies and milk
left out for me

I was almost finished with my Christmas Eve deliveries when I ran out of candy canes! What's a jolly old elf to do? Then I remembered an all-night candy-cane factory. They loaded up my sleigh in five minutes—and gave me some rejects for free! Can you find these funny-shaped candy canes? And can you find me?

S-shaped

Pretzel-shaped

Checkered

Figure-8

Two-headed

Coiled

Square

Diamond

Double-ended

RECYCLE

VENDING MACHINE

PEPPERMINT MILKSHAKES

CANDY CANE COLA

MINT HOT CHOCOLATE

CHOCOLATE MINT BARS

PEPPERMINT ICE CREAM

WHAT'S BLACK AND WHITE AND RED ALL OVER?

DON'T FORGET TO BRUSH

CANDY CANE FACTORY

SYSTEM OVERLOAD

THE CHRISTMAS PARTY LINER

THE TINY TIM

Most people think I only fly through the air to deliver Christmas gifts. The mermaids, mermen, and other sea creatures will tell you differently. In fact, I swim so well, they think I'm one of them! Can you find me? Can you find this other silly sea stuff?

A Christmas seal

A hammerhead shark

All eight of my reindeer

An angelfish

A catfish

A peanut-butter-and-jellyfish

5 notes in a bottle

A submarine

ROBINSON CRUSOE

TITANIC

DEAR SANDY CLAWS PLEASE GIVE ME A
1.
2.
3.

I had "wrapped up" my Christmas Eve rounds when I realized I hadn't wrapped my gift to Mrs. Claus yet! I stopped at Worldwide Gift Wrap, Inc., to see if they could help me out. Boy, were they busy! I decided to wrap Mrs. Claus's fuzzy slippers myself. After you find me, see if you can find these things that will help me wrap my gift.

A green shoebox

A stapler

A red ruler

Candy-cane wrapping paper

A green tape dispenser

A snowman card

A pair of yellow scissors

A pencil

CARDS & TAGS DEPARTMENT
RIBBONS & BOWS DEPARTMENT

MERRY CHRISTMAS

BOWS

WORLDWIDE GIFT WRAP, INC.

GIFT WRAP WHILE-U-WAIT

SNACK BAR

BOSS'S OFFICE

BOX DEPARTMENT

PAPER-PRINTING PRESSES

Mrs. Claus thinks I've put on a little weight lately. She suggested I take up skiing and skating. The ski lessons were fun, but it went downhill after that! After you find me, see if you can find all of these other silly skiers and skaters.

A skier in a fur coat

A real cool dude

"Duck!"

Wroger Wrongway

Somebody who's all "wrapped up" in skiing

A skier who's "out of this world!"

A real rockin' skier

A figure skater

Grab your wallet and head back into the craft show! Can you find these silly things?

☐ A runaway gingerbread man
☐ A "door" prize
☐ A pickpocket plant
☐ Paul Bunyan's mom
☐ A pig in a blanket
☐ Pinocchio
☐ A real fruit cake
☐ A vampire

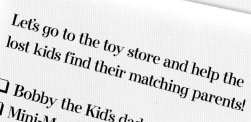

Let's go to the toy store and help the lost kids find their matching parents!

☐ Bobby the Kid's dad
☐ Mini-Muscle's dad
☐ Drummond Bugle's dad
☐ I. Wright Ticketts's mom
☐ Lil' Topknot's mom
☐ Mona Lisa's dad
☐ Chuckles and Giggle's's parents
☐ Presto's parents
☐ Hi Long Leggs's dad

Things are really hopping at the shopping mall! Go back and find these other crazy things:

☐ A tortoise racing a hare
☐ Music soothing the savage beast
☐ A jealous musician
☐ An indoor snowfall
☐ Dorothy's slippers
☐ The Three Little Pigs
☐ A bunny wearing people slippers

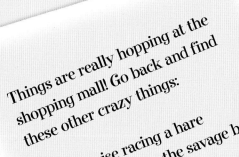

Take a closer look at Santa's workshop to see these funny things:

☐ A giant pan of Christmas cookies
☐ An elf tied to the train tracks
☐ A dog stealing a dolly
☐ A mouse running up a clock
☐ An elf who's the "target" of a prank
☐ A cowboy riding a reindeer
☐ A railroad "block"-ade

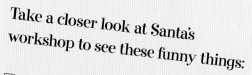